Richard Cumberland

The Mysterious Husband

A Tragedy in Five Acts

Richard Cumberland

The Mysterious Husband
A Tragedy in Five Acts

ISBN/EAN: 9783337069575

Printed in Europe, USA, Canada, Australia, Japan

Cover: Foto ©Andreas Hilbeck / pixelio.de

More available books at **www.hansebooks.com**

THE

MYSTERIOUS HUSBAND:

A TRAGEDY.

THE

MYSTERIOUS HUSBAND:

A

T R A G E D Y.

IN FIVE ACTS.

AS IT IS ACTED AT THE

THEATRE-ROYAL, COVENT-GARDEN.

———

By RICHARD CUMBERLAND, Esq.

———

D U B L I N:

PRINTED BY WILLIAM GILBERT,

M DCC LXXXV.

PROLOGUE.

DEEP in a labyrinth, remote from view,
Fame's temple ſtands, and Faſhion holds the clue:
Before the entrance rang'd, a ſuppliant band
Of candidates invoke her guiding hand :
In burſts the throng, a thouſand different ways
They ſpread, wind, double thro' the puzzling maze :
Vain labour his who on himſelf relies,
Where none but Faſhion's favorites gain the prize !

Sad omen for our poet ! who has choſe
The narrow groveling path of humble proſe ;
A path indeed, which Moore and Lillo trode,
And reach'd Parnaſſus by the bridle road :
Brambles and thorns oppoſe, and at our ſide
Nature alone, and ſhe a naked guide.
Patrons of nature, from your tears impart
Balm to her wounds, and heal her at your heart.

Now parody has vented all its ſpite,
Let tragedy reſume her antient right :
When Britain's lion roars in martial mood,
Throw to the kingly beaſt a ſop of blood ;
Loud in his ear your tragic thunders roll,
And rouſe the mighty terrors of his ſoul :
When peace, with every liberal ſcience join'd,
Decrees a joyful ſabbath to mankind,
Let comedy reſtore the court of wit,
And open a new ſeſſions in the pit.

Pageants and Pantomimes have ſpent their rage,
And emptied the whole wardrobe on the ſtage :
Lord Mayors of London clubb'd with Gods of Greece,
And Biſhop Blaize comb'd Jaſon's golden fleece ;
Whilſt ſlipſhod taylors on their treſſel boards,
Of the Nine Muſes ſate the croſs-legg'd lords ;
Let a plain bard, in ſpite of Faſhion, aim,
By Nature's aid, to find his way to fame :
To his domeſtic tale incline your ear,
Wives, huſbands, children ! you may ſafely hear.

A 3

Dramatis Personæ.

Lord Davenant	-	Mr. HENDERSON.
Charles Davenant	-	Mr. LEWIS.
Sir Edmund Travers		Mr. YATES.
Captain Dormer	-	Mr. WROUGHTON.
Sir Harry Harlow		Mr. AIKIN.
Paget - - - -		Mr. FEARON.
Lady Davenant	-	Miſs YOUNGE.
Marianne - - -		Miſs SATCHELL.
Waiting Woman - -		Miſs PLATT.

Lord Davenant's Servants, &c.

TIME, *the Repreſentation.*

SCENE, LONDON.

The Mysterious Husband:

A TRAGEDY.

ACT I.

SCENE I. *An Apartment in* Lord Davenant's *House.*

Enter Lord Davenant.

Lord D. **D**ID ever man mistake his happiness as I have done? am I by nature fitted for a husband? am I by temper qualified to be a gamester? and yet (a plague upon my folly!) I am both: in both I've doubled stakes, and play'd the losing game; married a wife for money, and a wife for love; and now nor love nor money will get rid of either: upon my right hand and my left a plague; over-head ruin impends; under-foot lurks discovery. A situation that admits no choice, but choice of miseries. As to my Lady Davenant here, if ever man was punish'd in a faultless wife, it is

my

my fate to be that man; with beauty to attract, affections to assist temptation, still she stands upon a rock of virtue; nor can I, by the narrowest search, explore a crack or cranny, where the slightest levity might enter, to throw down her barriers, and make way for my escape:———when a wife's indiscretion will not save me, well may I rail at fortune; 'tis hard to lose upon a cast, where every chance was in my favour.———Now, Paget, before I talk to you, shut the door.

Enter Paget, and shuts the Door.

What have you discover'd in Lady Davenant since we last conferr'd?

PAGET. Nothing.

LORD D. No doubt you have watch'd her—

PAGET. Closely.

LORD D. Where has she been? whom has she seen? what has she done?

PAGET. The journal of one day is the journal of her life: if I had the eyes of a hawk (and mine are none of the dullest) I could not spy a flaw in Lady Davenant.

LORD D. Incredible! Are not you an attorney, and is not she a woman? have not I set you as a spy upon her person; cas'd the body of a lawyer in the livery of a servant; and, after three months past and more, will you persuade me, that you have discovered, what the world never knew, a wife without a flaw? I'll not believe it.

PAGET. Why then, my Lord, you must ev'n strip my livery off my back, and dismiss me to my parchments.

LORD D. You will find flaws enough in them: of this I'm sure, if any thing can outwit a lawyer, it must be the devil; therefore, Paget, I conclude against her Ladyship's sanctity. What do you tell me? has this great city lost its temptations, or reform'd its morals? There are a hundred fine men of the town, who say she is the finest woman in it.

PAGET.

PAGET. Yes; and swear it too: but she won't believe e'm.

LORD D. She was credulous enough, when I told her so.

PAGET. 'Twas a great weakness; but she is wiser than she was.

LORD D. Does Sir Harry Harlow make no way? He is a fashionable man, and came on with all the gallantry of a Frenchman.

PAGET. Yes, and went off like a Frenchman; he'll not rally any more; we have orders never to admit him——she is in frequent conversation with your son.

LORD D. I have remark'd it, and shall stop their interviews.

PAGET. She has been collecting a sum—

LORD D. What is that for?

PAGET. That's more than I can tell· I sold some trinkets for her of her uncle's giving, and exchanged some money into notes this morning.

LORD D. I paid her quarter's pin-money but yesterday:—this must be look'd into.

PAGET. Yes, we may look; but it is seeking for day-light with a dark-lanthorn: malice cannot spy a fault in her; mischief cannot make one; and if I might offer my advice, it should be to desist from any further pains in the attempt: 'tis merely loss of labour, take my word for it.

LORD D. To say the truth, I begin to be of your opinion; but till a better plan can be struck out, we must persist in this: you know my reasons, Paget; you alone, of all mankind, are in the secret of that fatal step, which trains me on in infamy and error. If Lady Davenant was in fact, as she is in law, my only wife, I would not act as now; but whilst that second marriage in Flanders with Miss Dormer draws off my heart, and keeps me under terror of discovery, if I can't find occasion for a divorce, I must make it.

PAGET. 'Tis plain your passion for Miss Dormer still subsists, else her persuasion of your death, her
ignorance

ignorance of your name and station, and the precautions we have taken to prevent discovery, make these measures needless.

Lord D. I wish I saw it in that light; but what security have I against Miss Dormer's coming over? what against her marrying again, believing, as she does, that I am dead?—that were a stroke that I should doubly feel. Another danger threatens me; her brother Dormer may return from sea: his former passion for my Lady Davenant, and gratitude for my services in getting him a ship, will expose me to his visits: and I would sooner meet the devil than the man I've wrong'd so deeply.

Paget. 'Twould not be pleasant, I confess; but surely 'twas reported he was kill'd in action with an enemy's ship in the East Indies.

Lord D. Wounded, not kill'd:—But hark! my Lady's coming.—Vanish! [*Exit Paget.* Good morning to you, Lady Davenant;—dress'd so early!

Enter Lady Davenant.

Lady D. 'Tis my uncle's day for visiting, and I made myself ready to receive him.

Lord D. Come, come, that studied elegance of dress can never be put on to receive an uncle; you had some better object in your eye than old Sir Edmund Travers.

Lady D. Perhaps I had.

Lord D. Why that's sincere; I know you do not set yourself in such array for family visitors.

Lady D. I own it; but a stranger, and a favourite too—when such a one is in the case—

Lord D. Ay, then you arm at every point for conquest: but this stranger—tell me, who is he?

Lady D. Who is a greater stranger than your Lordship? If I'm arm'd for conquest, here's the heart I aim at.

Lord D. Pshaw! this is trifling; these are words in course. If man and wife keep forms, 'tis
all

all that is requir'd; but to pretend a paffion, and talk of love to a hufband—'tis an affectation that lowers your underftanding, but cannot impofe upon mine. In the name of reafon, Lady Davenant, make yourfelf an agreeable wife, but do not fink into that moft infipid of all characters, a good fort of woman.

LADY D. And what is your defcription of a good fort of woman?

LORD D. She is one that keeps the commandments, hears fermons, talks a little innocent fcandal, and fcolds the fervants.

LADY D. Now tell me your receipt for an agreeable wife.

LORD D. An agreeable wife to a man of the world is a woman of the world; one who follows her own purfuits, and does not crofs thofe of her hufband. Let me fpeak to you with fincerity—we married for convenience; there is a difparity in our ages; I was a widower, with a fon as old as yourfelf; you an orphan girl of fortune, a flave to the humours of your uncle; you purchafed liberty by the facrifice of inclination.

LADY D. How does that appear, my Lord?

LORD D. Beyond a doubt; you know your heart was never mine; you know you was in love with Dormer; would have married him; was thwarted in your firft affection, and took me upon duty—I might have faid upon compulfion; for I was your uncle's choice, not yours.

LADY D. Hold there, whilft I declare to you, in truth of heart, if Dormer had not given me up,— unkindly given me up—it was not duty, no, nor yet compulfion, fhould have forced me to renounce him.

LORD D. I give you credit for a fair confeffion, and I draw this natural conclufion from it:—The woman who has loved, will love again—I am content. Let me fpeak plainly to you: you are young, handfome, fenfible, fufceptible: I am declining from the prime of life, a lover of my eafe, and, I

confefs

confefs to you, not over uxorious. ·Why fhould we reftrain each other? Why fhould marriage, that ftrikes off other women's fetters, put on your's? live as women of your rank live; let your life be neither that of a town·libertine, nor this, which you now lead, of a matrimonial mope.

LADY D. I underftand you, my Lord: but if I am better pleafed to fubmit to the chagrin of your negleft, than to the reproaches of my own confcience, you will fuffer me to purfue a dull choice, and be the objeft of your contempt, rather than of my own. I'll not difguife from you that my heart is made for love, foft and fubjeft to temptation, therefore I avoid it: it once belonged to Dormer; he returned it·wounded, bleeding to its owner; 'twas healed, made whole, and·offered to·Lord Davenant; if you will not receive it, you may fend it back to me, as Dormer did; but you fhall never make it common property, affure yourfelf.

·LORD·D. Well, let that pafs. I have a queftion, to which I beg your anfwer, without evafion or referve.

LADY D. Propofe it.

LORD D. ·What has ·paffed of ·late between your Ladyfhip and my fon? You have been clofetted more than once; what have you conferred upon?

.LADY D. Am·I·bound·to tell that?

.LORD D, Indifpenfably; I .charge you on your duty; if you will put yourfelf on your defence, defend yourfelf. I have remark'd a fullennefs in Captain Davenant, that does not pleafe me; a darknefs and referve not proper; and I fufpeft your.Ladyfhip of .being party.in .the occafion.

LADY D. No, no; if ever I am forc'd to make my forrows known, it will not be to your fon I fhall fpeak unfavourably of his father.

·LORD D. No matter; tell .me what pafs'd.

.LADY·D. ·Read then, and fatisfy your doubts.

[*Gives him a letter.*

LORD D.

LORD D. *(Reads)*

" Dear Charles,

" As it may be inconvenient to your father to fur-
" nish you with the purchase-money for your majo-
" rity, accept this trifle in aid from your ever af-
" fectionate,

" Louisa Davenant."

Confusion!———let me see; five hundred pounds!
———your Ladyship is very bountiful to Captain
Davenant; and very considerate, as you would have
it appear, of his father's pocket. If you had studied the neceffities of that, Madam, why might not
your bounty pass through my hands? how know
you I approve of this? how can you tell but other
calls may be more urgent with me than this of a
commiffion for my son? what if I have duns of honour now at my door? what if I have play-debts,
that cannot be put aside? will you unstring your
purse; empty your hoard of pin-money for me?—I
do not find you will.

LADY D. 'Tis in your hands; dispose of it 'as
you see fit.

LORD D. And I do see fit to dispose of mine
and my son's concerns without your Ladyship's advice or interference: I shall also expect, and strictly
require, that you do not talk and cabal with my son
upon any thing that now passes, ever did pass, or
ever shall pass, between you and me upon the subject.

Servant introduces Sir Edmund Travers.

SERV. Sir Edmund Travers.
SIR EDM. Lord Davenant, I kiss your hands—
why this is as it should be; this is as it us'd to be in
days of yore, when man and wife fulfill'd the saying
and were one flesh. I protest to you, I have been
let into the houses of three married couple this
morning, and found but one and a half at home.

B   LORD

Lord D. Perhaps the hen birds were on the perch, Sir Edmund.; 'tis rather early.

Sir Edm. Very good, very good, but that was not the case—Lady Turtle, for inſtance, was on the wing; that dove had left the ark;—knowing Sir Philander to be ſo fond a mate, I aſked him of my Lady—ſhe was not in the houſe—how did ſhe do? he could not tell—where was ſhe gone? he did not care—I ſtared at this—he obſerving my ſurprize, ſaid, he ſuppoſed I had not heard of his misfortune, elſe I would never have mentioned that vile huſſey in his hearing—a plague upon all family affairs! thought I; 'twas not a week ago, this fellow held me by the ear with a detail as tedious as the court-ſhip of Jacob and Rebecca—but I have always ſaid, Lord Davenant and my Niece are the only inſtances of conjugal felicity, in upper life at leaſt.

Lady D. If you think us ſo happy, Uncle, why don't you take an agreeable companion to cheer the evening of your days?

Sir Edm. To hang myſelf in the evening of my days: how cou'd you name ſo horrible a thing to me as an agreeable companion?

Lady D. I've obſerv'd, that they who rail moſt againſt matrimony, are the firſt to marry.

Sir Edm. And I've remark'd, that they who marry, are the firſt to rail: lack-a-day, if I did not find you and my Lord here together in a family way, as they call it, always civil and courteous to each other, with a ſmile of complacency on your countenances, what ſhould I think?—if I did not ſee theſe things with my own eyes, what ſhould I ſay, when ſo many buſy tattling fools are whiſpering it about that you are the moſt unhappy couple in London?

Lord D. Whiſpering, Sir Edmund! they'll whiſper any thing; but who dares ſay it?

Sir Edm. That was juſt my anſwer; my anſwer to a tittle:—a plague upon you all! ſaid I t'other night to a knot of old ſogrums at the Mount, who were caballing over their coffee, not perceiv-

ing

ing me fnug in a corner box—a plague upon you
all! faid I—

Lord D. Tedious old blockhead!—I'll efcape
in time.   [*Going.*

Sir Edm. My Lord, my lord, hear out my ftory;
it is told in three words.

Lord D. I beg your pardon, but I've indif-
penfable bufinefs, and have outftaid my engagement.   [*Exit Lord Davenant.*

Sir Edm. Why look you there, now—'tis fur-
prizing how unwilling people are to hear my ftories;
not a man in our club will fit them out, except the
fmoakers. 'Twas juft the fame, when I was in Par-
liament, nothing but coughing, hemming, and fhuf-
fling of feet: no attention, no defire of information:
all their brains a gadding. And your Lord has a
piece of that, let me tell you; but a good man in
the main, an excellent man in the main, an incom-
parable hufband.—

Lady D. I make no complaint.

Sir Edm. To be fure you don't—complaint indeed! no, if you had the leaft caufe for that, truft
me for finding it out; nothing of that fort could efcape me, you know it could not.

Lady D. I fhould be forry you had any caufe to
regret a match fo entirely of your own making.

Sir Edm. Right, child, you are right; 'twas
a match of my own making; you owe all your hap-
pinefs to your uncle; and you now perceive a grey
head was a little wifer than a green one: you was
once of another opinion, but that's paft and over; I
don't reproach you, Louifa; indeed I may charge
that error of your life to my own indulgence. I hu-
mour'd you to a fault in your education; turn'd my
houfe into a fchool to make you happy; let you
have as many mafters as you pleas'd; doctors and
apothecaries, you might choofe amongft them all;
but in the important article of a hufband, there indeed I ftept in, there I had my choice, as was natural
I fhould; and now you fee the confequence; now,
Louifa, I fay, you fee the confequence.

Lady

LADY D. I do indeed, Sir.

SIR EDM. Why that's fair;. you are perfectly happy, and you own it, that's sincere: and what did I do to make you so? thwarted your inclinations, that were leading you astray.: I chose my Lord Davenant here, a man of a certain age, a widower, d'ye see.; not only fit to husband you, Louisa, but to father you; whereas you know, and, if you are honest, you will confess, that if I had indulg'd you in your choice—

LADY D. I should have chosen otherwise.

SIR EDM. You would have married young Dormer.

LADY D. I confess it.

SIR EDM. Oh, the many anxious thoughts I had to prevent it! how did I puzzle my poor brain to make you happy, and break off your connexion with that young fellow!

LADY D. Was there a contrivance in that business?

SIR EDM. Was there a contrivance, child! to be sure there was; there's a contrivance in every thing I do: and I must do Lord Davenant the justice to say, he took some pains in that affair as well as myself—witness Captain Dormer's letter to you.—

LADY D. What of that, I beseech you? let me know all my obligations to Lord Davenant.

SIR EDM. And 'tis fit you should; every man's good deeds should be known; he wrote every word of that letter himself; not a syllable was Captain Dormer's.

LADY D. Not a syllable!

SIR EDM. Not a tittle—and my Lord never told you this?—

LADY D. Never.

SIR EDM. That's extraordinary; but indeed he bound me to secrecy; so you must say nothing of the matter: oh! he was at uncommon pains for your sake; for he thought you would be a monstrous fortune; and to be sure you will at my death—but

there

there I outwitted him too, for I came down with only ten thousand, and saddled him with a humming jointure, and four hundred a year pin-money. —Ah, my dear Louisa, I consulted your happiness in every tittle of your settlement.

LADY D. Since you have been so considerate of me in the bargain you have made with Lord Davenant, let me hope you will now assist him in a family difficulty. His son is treating for the purchase of a majority, and wants a sum of money to complete it; he is an excellent young man, and you would do me a most acceptable kindness, if you would enable me to supply him with five hundred pounds.

SIR EDM. Ah Louisa, Louisa! I'm afraid the stories I've heard of your husband's gaming are too true.

LADY D. About as true as what you've heard of our unhappiness: but I thought you treated all such reports with contempt.

SIR EDM. And so I do—but time flies; 'tis visiting day with me, and I must leave you—good morning.

LADY D. But you have given me no answer about the money.

SIR EDM. Answer, child! what signifies answering you, when the thing is impossible.

[*Exit.*

Lady Davenant.

So then it seems I have been dup'd by base contrivances:—Dormer is clear, and I am sacrific'd. Lord Davenant's conduct is compleat; begins with treachery and ends in tyranny. Most miserable of women, to whom shall I complain?—it is too much; I can't support my agony.

[*Throws herself on a couch and weeps.*

Sir Edmund re-enters.

SIR EDM. Ay, now she's crying, because I refus'd her the money: what a fond fool it is! I warrant now she'd pledge her diamonds to redeem her husband—

LADY D. Who's there?

SIR EDM. 'Tis I, 'tis uncle Edmund. Nay, Louisa, if you cry, 'tis all over with me;—take the money, give me a kiss—I am a foolish fond old fellow, and cannot bear to see you unhappy. If 'twere as much again, you should have it; but don't ask me for any more, I pray you don't. 'Tis all in notes; they would have been navy bills before night—but I'm a foolish fond old fellow, that's the truth of it.

LADY D. I thank you, Sir, I thank you.

SIR EDM. A propos! here is the very gentleman you was speaking of. Come in, Captain Davenant; come in without ceremony: my lady has got something for you, but I tell no tales, I betray no secrets—so, so; I leave you together. Good bye to you. I leave you together. [*Exit.*

Enter Captain Davenant.

CAPT. D. What is this secret that Sir Edmund has broach'd? what commands has your Ladyship for me?

LADY D. After what my uncle has said, 'tis in vain to deny that I have a request to make, which I beg you not to refuse me.

CAPT. D. If the request shall be, as I suspect it is, to receive fresh favours from you, 'tis the only difficulty you can put me to in obeying you.

LADY D. If you knew what pleasure I receive by tendering to you this trifle towards the purchase of your rank, you would take it for my sake without further scruple: if you have any regard for me, accept it at my hands.

CAPT. D. What shall I say to you, most generous of women?

LADY

LADY D. Nothing; neither is it convenient, we should converse together: I am obliged to request of you not to mention what has pass'd.

CAPT. D. O Lady Davenant! Lady Davenant! my heart bleeds for you———

LADY D. Hush! not a word of that———now, Sir———

Enter Servant.

SERV. Sir Harry Harlow to wait upon your Ladyship.

LADY D. Did not I tell you to deny me? I am not at home to Sir Harry Harlow.   [*Exit.*

SERV. What wou'd your honour please to have me do? he is coming up stairs.

CAPT. D. Rascal, begone!   [*Exit Servant.*

Sir Harry Harlow.

SIR H. H. How now, Charles! rating the footman? it is indeed an untowardly whelp; her Ladyship is not very select in the choice of her lacqueys; he wou'd have persuaded me I was not to be let in.———But won't your fair mother-in-law make her appearance?

CAPT. D. No.

SIR H. H. No, man! is that all the answer you can afford me! the yard-dog wou'd say as much.

CAPT. D. Take your answer from him then, when you make your next enquiries.

Enter Lord Davenant.

LORD D. How now, Gentlemen both, at sharps with each other?

SIR H. H. Captain Davenant seems to guard your Lordship's doors, as if it was a crime to enter them; if so, I must confess it is a crime I am not disposed to repent of, at least till you tell me I ought to do so.   [*Capt. Davenant walks aside.*

LORD D,

Lord D. Pooh! 'tis his manner; 'tis the fashion of the times: the young men now-a-days, and the young women too, talk no other language to their dearest friends.——Hark ye, Charles, have the kindness to step into the library; I want a few words in private with you.

[*Exit Capt. Davenant.*

This young man has ruffled you; and, to say truth, his manners are much alter'd: whether he mistakes in thinking a fierce military air becomes him, or that some secret matter really disconcerts him, I can't pretend to say, for he communicates with me but little: I beg you will think no more of what is past for my sake.

Sir H. H. Assure yourself, my Lord, 'tis as if it had never been.

Lord D. Here, Harry, I have a play debt to settle with you; take these notes.

Sir H. H. As you will for that; chuse your own time.

Lord D. Nay, but take them;——'twas a cursed crash I got last night.   [*Gives him the Notes.*

Sir H. H. Deuce take me, my Lord, if it does not go to my heart to win your money: I have a thousand times resolv'd never to play with you again.

Lord D. Why so in the name of wonder?

Sir H. H. Because I cannot bear to wear in my pocket what might so much better be employ'd elsewhere.

Lord D. What is the man moralizing about?

Sir H. H. Well, I protest and vow, was I the husband of Lady Davenant——

Lord D. You wou'd be as tir'd of her as I am.

Sir H. H. For shame, for shame! what woman can be more engaging?

Lord D. Every woman that is not my wife.

Sir H. H. That ever matrimony shou'd bring a man to this!——as Heaven shall be my judge, I'd give one half of my estate to share the other with the woman you are so indifferent about.

Lord D. And I wou'd give this arm from off this body to be quit of her; so there's the difference between you and me: but let us talk no more of the subject——is your chariot in waiting?

Sir H. H. It is.

Lord D. Are you going to any distance?

Sir H. H. Only to a visit in the next street, and then home.

Lord D. If that's all, I should be glad you wou'd take my chair, and lend me your carriage; I have a little business at t'other end of the town.

Sir H. H. Take it where you please; 'tis at your service: I perceive I shall not have the honour of making my bow to Lady Davenant this morning.

Lord D. To say the truth, I suspect you will not: it does not appear to me, Harry, that you are in train to make your way to her Ladyship's good graces;——and it requires a very moderate share of resolution to resist temptation, where there is no inclination for the tempter.

End of the first A C T.

ACT

A C T II.

An Apartment in Lord Davenant's *House.*

Lady Davenant, followed by Captain Davenant.

CAPT. D. I Muſt ſpeak to you: you muſt give me a few minutes hearing.

LADY D. Promiſe then, you will not name your father.

CAPT. D. 'Tis upon another buſineſs quite; an dbecauſe you are the friend I beſt love on earth, you ſhall be the firſt to whom I communicate my joy.

LADY D. You have obtained your commiſſion?

CAPT. D. I have indeed, but not the commiſ-fion, my dear Lady, you are thinking of; not a promotion to rank, but to happineſs——I am married.

LADY D. Heaven and earth!——to whom?

CAPT. D An angel: one, who in mind and perſon is your ſiſter; and, if evil fate had not for-bade, might have been ſuch in fact.

LADY D. What do you mean? explain your-ſelf.

CAPT. D: The ſiſter of your Dormer.

LADY D. My Dormer!—What is it you tell me?—does your father know of this?

CAPT. D. It is not fit he ſhould : how could he be reconcil'd to my choice, when he neglects his own?

LADY D. Remember your promiſe, and no more of this——Where did you meet Miſs Dormer? I thought ſhe was reſident in Flanders.

CAPT. D. 'Twas there I met her, on my late journey to Spa:——how I became acquainted with her; why I conceal'd from you my paſſion; with each circumſtance of her affecting ſtory, will de-mand

mand relation more at large —— but she is not, as you call her, Miss Dormer.

LADY D. That I can readily conceive, since you have married her.

CAPT. D. But she was not. Miss Dormer when I did marry her: she was the widow of an English gentleman, of the name of Brooke, who liv'd with her about three months; went to Paris, and there died :—— there is something mysterious in the conduct of this man; but that, with other matters, I must now defer. We are just return'd from a church in the city; but as friendship has its claim upon my heart as well as love, I snatch an hour from my enchanting bride to seek her counterpart; and, as I fear you have few blessings you can call your own, I beg you to accept a share of mine.—— Farewell!

LADY D. May happiness attend you both!

[*Exit Capt. Davenant.*

Married to Dormer's sister! How that name strikes on my heart!——And I the confidante of a clandestine marriage :—— a dangerous secret for my peace; the transport of the moment never suffered him to think of that—— well, let the danger come!—— there was a time I shou'd have been more scrupulous; but the base conduct of Lord Davenant makes him loathsome in my eyes; and was my injur'd hero now to come——Oh, Heaven, I will not think of it——Watch over him, ye guardians of the good and brave!—— waft him, ye winds, to glory!—— may the ship that bears him, and the star by which he sails, be ever prosperous!—— and, as he walks the deck by night, amidst the waste of waters, should a thought of my unkindness smite his manly heart with sadness, may some pitying spirit turn aside the thought, and strike out my unhappy name from his remembrance!

Enter Servant.

SERV. Please your Ladyship, there is a seaofficer below, enquires for my Lord; I told him
he

he was from home, but he says he will wait his
return.

LADY D. Where is my Lord?

SERV. Gone out in Sir Harry Harlow's chariot:
I hope his Lordship will not be angry at my letting
the gentleman in.

LADY D. I hope not; you should make him give
his name, however.

SERV. That I did at first, Madam; 'tis our
general order.

LADY D. And what is his name?

SERV. He has wrote it down on a card——Blefs
me, my Lady! something's the matter; shall I run
for your Ladyship's woman?

LADY D. No, no, be quiet—it will go off—
what have I done with the card?

SERV. Here it is: pray, my Lady, forgive my
boldness, and let me call your servant.

LADY D. There's no occasion;—I charge you
not to mention to a soul that I was ill—Shew the
gentleman into the eating-parlour—and remember
to tell nobody of this trifling disorder.

SERV. Not for the world——The blessing pn
her! what a sweet Lady it is?   [*Exit.*

Lady Davenant.

LADY D.—Dormer return'd, and in the house!
All-ruling Providence, receive a helpless creature
into thy protection! succour my fainting spirits in
this dangerous moment, and support my resolution,
struggling in a tide of passions, from whose overwhelming force no hand but thine can save me!—I
obey—it is thy voice that warns me to avoid him;
and tho' to justify myself to Dormer were the dearest object of my life, I will not do it: no, let me
suffer as I may, I will not meet him; I will never
see him more.

Enter

Enter Waiting Woman.

W. Wom. O Madam! O my Lady! such a thing is come to pass! Captain Dormer's in the house; I have seen him with my own eyes.

Lady D. Well, if he is, what's that to me? was it well done of you, to expose me by your idle curiosity?

W. Wom. Indeed and indeed, my Lady, I was innocently going into the eating-parlour for your Ladyship's netting-box, not thinking any body was there, when I saw a sea-officer in his uniform, looking earnestly at your Ladyship's portrait over the chimney; his back was towards me, so I did not know who it was; and on I went, thinking no offence, when suddenly he turn'd upon me; and then to be sure I gave a loud shriek, discovering him to be Captain Dormer.

Lady D. Does he know I am in this house?

W. Wom. Know, Madam! to be sure he knows your Ladyship is married to my Lord; for he ask'd me if the portrait was not drawn for you, which you know I cou'd not deny;—and then he ask'd me how it came in this house, and so I told him you was married to my Lord, which is nothing but the truth—and then, mercy on me, how he started! so I thought I wou'd say no more; but as I was going, Madam, he took me by the hand and held me, and then he ask'd me half a hundred questions, all in a breath, so that I knew not what to answer; but telling him that your Ladyship wanted me up stairs, away I run—and if I have done any thing amiss, I heartily ask your Ladyship's pardon.

Lady D. Amiss! I know not what you've done. Did he ask to see me?

W. Wom. Oh! most earnestly; but I was afraid to tell your Ladyship of that; indeed he beg'd very hard to see you.

Lady D. Impossible! It must not be.—How does he look?

W. Wom. Lovelily; you wou'd be charm'd to see him.

C

LADY

Lady D. Pooh!—I mean is he in health?

W. Wom. In perfect health.

Lady D. Thank Heaven for that!

W. Wom. Madam?

Lady D. Restrain your curiosity, if you please, and say nothing of what has pass'd. Go down to Captain Dormer, and tell him—tell him I am rejoic'd—No, that won't do—Cruel necessity?—Tell him I must never see him more.

W. Wom. Lack-a-day, my Lady, I shall never have the heart to tell him that—Oh, the mischief! here's my Lord.   [*Exit hastily.*

Enter Lord Davenant.

Lord D. So your Captain Dormer is come home, and you have admitted him into my house.

Lady D. No, my Lord, I have not admitted him.

Lord D. But your ambassadress there has been in treaty:—messages have passed; I know they have.

Lady D. My conduct, my Lord, is open; I have no secrets, and if it is any satisfaction to you to know it, I can assure you it is my fixt resolution never to see Captain Dormer any more.

Lord D. A woman's resolution; and you'll keep it accordingly.

Lady D. I hope I shall keep it for your Lordship's sake as well as my own.

Lord D. For my sake!

Lady D. Yes, I have the strongest reasons on your account. Captain Dormer is an injur'd man; interviews might draw on explanations, and these might lead to consequences of an unpleasant nature.

Lord D. You deal in riddles, Madam; your tone is rais'd too, now your champion's in the house.

Enter

Enter Servant.

SERV. Captain Dormer's compliments, and begs to know if your Lordship will be pleas'd to see him.

LORD D. Tell him I'll wait upon him presently —[*Exit Servant*] What can she mean by explanations?—her confidence alarms me—if Paget has betray'd me—if she has heard of my affair with Dormer's sister, all is lost.—I'll prove her further. [*Aside.*] You say that Dormer is an injur'd man; who tells you so? what is his injury, and who has done it?

LADY D. If letters have been fabricated which he never wrote; and if it may be call'd an injury to impress with false opinions hearts that were once devoted to each other, then am I warranted in what I say:—My uncle is my author.

LORD D. So your wife uncle has told you this;—this is the mighty mystery—for my share of the artifice, it is amongst the crimes I have repented of most cordially: You cannot execrate the luckless hour that made us one more bitterly than I do.

LADY D. Since it is so, my Lord, I shall not aggravate that bitterness by exposing you to the reproaches of Captain Dormer.

LORD D. If you've no other reason for avoiding him but this, you are free to justify yourself at my expence;—if you have nothing else to charge me with to Captain Dormer, this I can face, and instantly—Who waits?—nay, I'll prevent you, own to what I've done, and stand by consequences, be they what they may—Stay, you yourself shall hear me.

LADY D. I beg to be excus'd: I must insist upon permission to withdraw.

Enter Servant.

LORD D. Tell Captain Dormer I am ready to receive him—for if the time must come when he

C 2   that

that does the wrong, and he that suffers it, shall face to face bring their accounts to issue, better that the audit pass in this life than another—Why then this sudden tremor?—conscience, conscience, is this fair dealing? slow to admonish, when you might have sav'd me; loud in reproach, when admonition is too late. What if I told this young man all the wrong I've done him?——what if I avow'd the horrid injury that's yet unknown; that worm that gnaws my heart; that canker, which the incision of his sword can only cure?——I know the awful consummation is at hand: I feel the coming on of things; but when, and in what manner they shall pass, I cannot tell. The hand that rules my fate must fashion it.

Servant introduces Captain Dormer.

Serv. Captain Dormer.   [*Exit.*

Lord D. You are welcome to England, Sir: I am sorry I was not ready to receive you, and that you have been put to the trouble of waiting for me.

Dorm. The apology is due for my importunity, but I consider this as a visit of duty; and as I owe my command to your Lordship's recommendation, I was determin'd that the first door I enter'd in London should be your's.

Lord D. You are just arriv'd?

Dorm. Within this hour.

Lord D. You do me honour, and I hear with much content you've done yourself great honour, and the service.

Dorm. Such men and officers as I have serv'd with must ensure success; I must have been the sole defaulter in my ship, if we had flinch'd our duty.

Lord D. If there is any thing I can further obey you in, you will be pleas'd to command me.

Dorm. I humbly thank you; and can only say, tho' I have been long at sea, I don't wish to be idle on shore. There is a business, however, that I have at heart to settle before I go out again; and as your Lordship's favour has enabled me to make a fortune, the

the same friendship perhaps will assist me in the disposal of it.

LORD D. Explain yourself if you please; you know I have been always at your service.

DORM. I have a sister—

LORD. D. Sir!—[*Staring,*]

DORM. My Lord, I hope you have heard nothing to the contrary.

LORD. D. No; on my honour—please to proceed.

DORM. I hope she is yet living; 'tis a long time since I heard from her; she is the only relation I have left; an orphan girl, My Lord; and if she is still at Antwerp, where I left her, I can scarce hope to see her before I am order'd out again. To her I have bequeath'd the earnings of my service; and in the mean time made suitable provision for her support:—if you, who are the founder of my fortune, will kindly undertake this friendly trust, and suffer me to deposite in your care an orphan charge, you will put me under everlasting obligation.

LORD D. By Heaven, this is to much! [*Aside.*] Sir!—Mr. Dormer!—I am sensible of the honour you do me—but you must think I am a man not used to business of this sort—the commission is a very delicate commission:—the charge of a young lady—

DORM. Is a very sacred charge—I feel it such; and therefore ardently would wish to rest it with a man of honour. I am sensible of my presumption; I know I am imposing trouble, where I ought only to be paying gratitude;—but, my Lord, Davenant, I have no friends except in my own profession; they cannot serve me on this occasion. You are my only hope; and, as you have once taken me by the hand, I pray you do not let it go: I am bold to hope I shall not bring discredit on your protection, and I shall be through life devoted to you for the favour.

LORD. D. I am distressed; and if I do not answer you to your wish, it is because I'm sensible I do not merit the good opinion you repose in me:—you will allow me some time to reflect on what you desire.

C 3   DORM.

Dorm. By all means: I would not take your friendship by surprize. One thing I should naturally have stated to you before; but since I entered your Lordship's house, I have been informed of a circumstance, that makes the mention of it a matter of some embarrassment.

Lord D. What may that circumstance be?

Dorm. I understand you have the happiness to call a Lady your's whom I had once the audacity to aspire to;—Miss Travers I am told is Lady Davenaht.

Lord D. How is she interested in this business?

Dorm. Your Lordship having been privy to my passion for your most amiable Lady, I may be allowed to say to you, that it was my first passion, and will be my last. Her uncle's opposition, and her better destiny, traversed my too ambitious hopes, and reserved her to a worthier choice. Though there was something harder than I could have expected in her manner of dismissing me, still, upon reflection, I cannot condemn the Lady, who had prudence to reject an insolent pretender with the scorn he merited: nay, I am vain enough to flatter myself, her uncle dictated expressions that did not originate with her:—be that as it may, I have bequeathed my fortune to her upon failure of my sister and her heirs.

Lord. D. Astonishing! when did you take this resolution?

Dorm. When I was far enough from thinking I should ever see her more; after the action, when I was despaired of from my wounds: and though I do not wish your Lordship to report this to Lady Davenant, I hope it will be a motive with you for undertaking the trust, when so dear a part of you has an eventual interest in it.

Lord D. So dear a part of me! 'Tis plain that she is such to you; and her refusal has not yet extinguished your affection.

Dorm. No, my Lord, her honour and her happiness are still as dear to me as my own; no other object can ever interpose to draw off my attachment:

tachment: having once had the honour of being regarded by her, I can never defcend to think of any other woman; and I hope I have already convinced your Lordfhip, that, fo far from bearing enmity to the happy man who poffeffes her, I rejoyce to find that the object of her love and the friend of my life is one and the fame perfon. I therefore once again entreat you to take my fifter alfo into your protection; and you will then have in charge every thing I hold valuable on earth.

Lord D. This is really fo extraordinary, that I muft wonder on what grounds you reft a confidence in me fo full and fo implicit.

Dorm. To fay the truth, I follow Lady Davenant's choice; perfuaded I may truft my interefts where fhe repofes hers.

Lord D. But fuppofe, for a moment, that compulfion and not choice, determined Lady Davenant to ally herfelf to me.

Dorm. Impoffible! I'll not fuppofe it for a moment.

Lord D. Nay, let me put a ftronger cafe—— Suppofe this idol of your foul fhould raife no ecftacies in mine——What if this angel of perfection fhould to me appear the moft indifferent of women? ——In plainer words, what would you fay, if Lady Davenant was the object of my fix'd averfion?

Dorm. What would you fay! ——but I forbear, and underftand fuch fuppofitions as civil intimation that 'tis time I took my leave

Lord D. Oh, by no means: I've much to fay to you.

Dorm. Some other time: I've troubled you too long already.   [*Exit haftily.*

Lord Davenant.

Lord D. Curfed be the hour in which I wrong'd this man! What a clear fpirit! what a lofty foul! There is a ftatelinefs and grace in virtue, which
guilty

guilty pride can never imitate——'Sdeath! how I loath myself!——Damnation! what a wretch I am? If I had worlds I'd give them to be free.——Vain lamentation! vain remorse!——let no man think to take one step in infamy, and then retract:—— Impossible! the precipice has no degrees;—— down, down he falls at once, plunges into the fathomless abyss, and sinks for ever! [*Exit.*

SCENE *changes to the Apartment of* Marianne.

Marianne enters hastily.

MAR. Where shall I hide myself? He's in the house:——What shall I say——How shall I bear to see him?——Wretched, wretched woman! [*Weeps.*

Enter Charles to her.

CAPT. D. Joy to my Marianne! my wife! my——Heaven defend me! what's the matter? Why are you in tears?——My life! my soul! what ails thee?——Answer me, or I shall sink with apprehension.

MAR. Alas, my dearest friend, no more my husband——

CAPT. D. What do you mean? I am in agonies.

MAR. My husband is alive; I have seen him.

CAPT. D. What then am I?

MAR. Ruin'd, disgrac'd, betray'd;——and I the cause.

CAPT. D. Oh, insupportable and killing stroke! can there be misery more deep than this? By Heaven I'll not resign you. Villain, deceiver as he is, he cannot claim what he has faithlessly abandon'd; and, if he does, my sword shall strike him dead. Blast him, eternal justice!——burst underneath his feet, and swallow him, thou violated earth!

MAR.

Mar. By this our last embrace, I do beseech you moderate your rage ; it frightens me ; your looks are wild ;——have patience, and collect yourself to bear this cruel stroke.

Capt. D. If what extinguishes my happiness, deprives me of my reason, can I help it? if you have you seen him, known him, and convers'd with him, direct me where he is, and I'll assert my right ; for if he was my father, by the Power that made me——

Mar. Pray no more: hear me if possible, with some composure.

Capt. D. Where did this meeting pass? you have not left the house.

Mar. I saw him from my window in his chariot; there was a noise and uproar in the street; some fray between his servants and the Driver of a hackney Carriage——he had let down the glass, and stopt his chariot.

Capt. But are you sure 'twas he ?

Mar. Too sure : no sooner did my eye glance on his person, than terror struck, and scarce myself, I ran down to the door, went out, and call'd to him to stop, for now the carriages were disengag'd——

Capt. D. What did he then ?

Mar. He stopt, lookt out, discover'd me, and called eagerly to his coachman, drove furiously away.

Capt. D. Infamous wretch! abuser of your unprotected innocence! hypocrite, that counterfeiting piety, stole into the sanctuary of virtue, and robb'd the altar of its holiest relick——I never lik'd his story; always thought his sanctified approaches, under cloak of mock benevolence and pity, were suspicious: then this pretended death, and the inscrutable darkness succeeding it, were proofs demonstrative of fraud. My life upon't, he is some titled profligate. Have you no marks to trace him by? the equipage, arms, liveries? did you not note them?——through the earth I will pursue him to detection.

Mar.

Mar. I was incapable of such remarks: I have sent my servant amongst the neighbours; his equipage was gay and splendid, and 'tis possible it may be known——but what ensues, when it is known?——distraction, death.——Oh, leave me, Charles; renounce me, banish my misfortunes from your thoughts, and may some happier woman——

Capt. D. Madness is in the thought: never will I forsake thee; never by all that's sacred, whilst I live, will I acknowledge any other wife: in thy embrace is centered all my happiness;——here, here, my lovely Marianne, I will both live and die.

Mar. Alas, my dearest Charles, altho' my soul doats on you, can I for your sake suffer it?——ought I for my own?

Capt. D. Are you not then my wife? who shall oppose it? Have you any other husband? Let the world's laws interpret as they may, by right of Heaven's decree you are mine: let him that forged the lye, fall by the lye. What if the records of his death were false?——you thought them true; and in persuasion of their truth, you married; therefore he's dead to you, tho' he survives to villainy;——the husband is extinct, tho' the imposter lives.

Mar. For me, who am the child of sorrow, friendless and obscure, the world's opinions are no rule of right; 'Heaven and my conscience give the Law to me——but oh! to sink your frame and fortune, bury all your splendid hopes, your active talents——it is not to be thought of: no, your friends, your family, your country claims you; misfortune is my birth-right; I am encompass'd with a sphere of wretchedness, and every one is blighted that approaches me: an orphan in the cradle; one brave youth, one dear beloved brother, was the cordial of my life——of him perhaps I am bereft.

Capt. D. No, Providence restores him to you, this sad accident so filled my thoughts, or I had soon-

er

er told you the good tidings of your brother.—Dormer's arriv'd,

MAR. Is he arriv'd?

CAPT. D. He is arriv'd, and crown'd with glory,
crowned with fortune: you are the sister of a hero,
who will stand recorded in his country's brightest
annals: interest might solicit your alliance; pride
might boast of it; even misers now might court the
sister of the wealthy Dormer.

MAR. Then I will not despair: amidst the
clouds and darkness of my fate, Heaven yet shall visit me with one bright gleam of hope.

CAPT. D. 'Yes, we shall still be happy; I feel
my spirits lighten; my love to you is not a brutal
heat; 'tis founded on the graces of your mind;
brighten'd, but not blinded, by the charms of your
person. I have no part to act; to Dormer, to my
father, to the world I will avow my claim; I'll seek
your brother, join him in dragging forth to light this
dark Mysterious husband. To this I pledge my
word; till this be done, however painful the sus-
pence, however dear the sacrifice, I am your friend,
not husband.—Come, come then, thou soft affliction,
quiet thy distracted thoughts—all things will yet be
well.

End of the Second ACT.

A C T III.

Enter Lord Davenant and Paget.

LORD D. I Tell you, 'tis impossible. I am be-
set, embay'd; broad, full-fac'd in-
famy now states upon me. If all the dæmons that are
leagu'd in mischief sate in council for my rescue,
Hell and its advocates have no resource to ward off
my detection.

PAGET.

PAGET. I would have had you thought of this before.

LORD D. Prythee forbear reproach! my own heart is sufficient for that office.—Where is my Lady?

PAGET. In her chamber.

LORD D. Alone?

PAGET. I think so.

LORD D. Would she were in her grave?—I'll think of that—the fight of Marrianne, the glimpse I snatcht this morning of her beauties, fatal altho' it be, has stir'd the flame afresh: it burns within me; horror cannot quench it;—Dormer's return, his presence, his reproaches can't extinguish it; not even his sword, tho' it transfixed my heart.—But I forget to ask you what intelligence you've gather'd, Am I discovered? is my name out in the affair?

PAGET. I do not find it is; and if you wish it should not, you must take instant measures with Sir Harry Harlow and his servants; his equipage is known by many, and will lead discovery to you.

LORD D. To him you mean—and that's to me, Can I set him in front, and skulk behind his friend-ship like a coward? will he permit it, think you? No—can I?—there's no evasion left—now, what's your business?

Enter Servant.

SERV. My Lord, Sir Edmund Travers is below.

LORD D. Admit him—doating blockhead! blind fool! that cannot see the Sun at noon, for that is not more glaring in it's full meridian, than the apparent misery that he is author of—begone [*Exit Paget.*

Sir Edmond Travers.

SIR EDM. My Lord, I've news for you.

LORD D. Dromer's arrived.

SIR

Sir Edm. How your wit jumps!

Lord D. I've news for you. A secret; but you'll keep it.

Sir Edm. Oh! upon honour!

Lord D. Nay, as you will, for this it is—we are two sorry knaves.

Sir Edm. Who! you and I?

Lord D. Exactly so: a pair as perfect as iniquity e'er match'd. We trick'd this marriage neatly; did we not?—fine cheats, to pass these letters off upon your niece and Dormer—neat forgeries they were; and precious gulls the lovers, to be trapp'd so readily. But you are secret now; true to the gang; you did not blab this to Lady Davenant?

Sir Edm. What do you mean? I blab it! I to Lady Davenant!

Lord D. You. If you dare, deny it.

Sir Edm. Deny it! no, I cannot absolutely deny it; but who could think she would be fool enough to broach it?

Lord D. The first that broach'd it was the fool. You've set the mischief running; now drain the bitter cup of your affliction to its lowest and its foulest dregs. Dormer shall know the plot, which hand in hand we've practis'd to deceive him. The passion which was dead in him shall rise again: I'll urge them on, inflame them to renew'd desires; and, when their stimulated hearts rush to forbidden transports, then, in that guilty moment, you and I, like brother villains, will steal in with silent steps, and feast upon the ruin we have made.

Sir Edm. Oh horrible! you'll not do this.

Lord D. Why not? such true-bred sons of wickedness as we are, have a luxury in mischief. What do you care? you hate your niece; I execrate my wife.

Sir Edm. Why you are mad sure; stark mad and raving. I hate my niece! you execrate your wife! I thought you were the fondest pair on earth; and for my niece!—

ᵥLORD D. You ſtole her from an honeſt man, and ſold her to a Lord. ·Now get you home: weigh theſe things well in your diſcerning mind; put truth in one ſcale, titles in the other; and, when you've ſtruck the balance, come and compare accounts with me, and we'll divide the gains.　　　　　　[*Exit.*

Sir Edmund Travers.

SIR EDM. 'Tis as I ſaid: the man's beſide him-ſelf; out of all line and compaſs of right reaſon: I ſaw it in his eyes: the moon's in the mad quarter. 'Tis jealouſy of Dormer: ſheer downright jealouſy, and nothing elſe: foregad, and that will do't as ſoon as any thing. He ſaid he'd tell the plot to Dormer, make them both deſperately in love afreſh, and put them together; a proof of jealouſy:—he ſaid, he execrated his wife; a proof he loves her: and what are love and jealouſy but madneſs? how his poor brains are tumbled topſy-turvy! I pity him at my heart. I muſt look ſharp, and watch this Dormer cloſely; if I diſcover them at their old tricks, I ſhall make bold to read this niece of mine a good round lecture: when ſo many heads are gone aſtray, 'tis lucky for the world that ſome folks have their wits about them.　　　　　　[*Exit.*

Lord Davenant returns.

LORD D. I will not live in torment; nor ſhall the preaching of pedantic churchmen fetter this free ſpirit in his body, when it is weary of its priſon. What know they of an hereafter more than we, who never prov'd it? all is ſpeculation in futurity; and he that travels on in miſery, in the hope or fear of what ſhall meet him at his journey's end, gives up his reaſon for a dream, and follows a blind guide he knows not whither, and he knows not why.

Enter

Enter Lady Davenant.

LADY D. I interrupt your meditations.

LORD D. You shall partake of them—Come, I shall probe your spirit; I shall bring you to confession ere we part: is it not a miserable life we have pass'd together? is it not a cursed one?

LADY D. It might have been more happy.

LORD D. How? what can make harmony of discord? how can two hearts be brought together, that so widely point asunder? will the weak bands of marriage draw them nearer? No, we were made by Heaven so adverse and unlike in our original construction, that we may safely set the rubrick at defiance, and without more process, part.

LADY D. Part!

LORD D. For ever.

LADY D. On what plea?

LORD D. The best and fairest—mutual aversion.

LADY D. Of what can you accuse me?

LORD D. Of hypocrisy, if you persist to live with me: who harbours with the thing he hates? what creature mates with its opposite? Nature protests against it. You hate me: come, I know you do, and you have cause.

LADY D. Remove that cause: break off from those bad courses that degrade a mind not naturally degenerate: 'twill be a worthier separation, a more laudable divorce than from an unoffending wife.

LORD D. What if I did, you cannot love me.

LADY D. Try: there is virtue in the experiment at least.

LORD D. You love young Dormer; in your soul you love him; what your foolish uncle has betray'd, endears him to you more than ever: what I now shall tell you, will augment that augmentation, and inflame affection into phrenzy.

LADY D. Stop then in time. By every sacred name I charge you to forbear: let me be miserable, but do not make me guilty.

LORD D.

LORD D. I mean to save you both from misery
and guilt ;—I have convers'd with Dormer ; he
adores you : defeated in his hopes, dismiss'd, and
by our artifices us'd most hardly, still he persists to
love you. Nay, the deluded generous youth, because I am your husband, even on me devolves his
friendship and affection : tenders to me the execu-
tion of his will—solicits me (oh wond'rous test of
confidence !) to take the guardianship of Marianne.

LADY D. Astonishing!

LORD D. Yes, 'twere astonishing, if you knew
all. [*Aside.*] Nay, there is more—he has bequeath'd
you his whole fortune at his sister's death. Now,
what think you of this man? now, Lady Davenant,
how do you feel your heart affected by these proofs
of unabating love ?

LADY D. Deeply, most deeply—yet not otherwise I hope than as becomes your wife.

LORD D. Hence with the name! hence with
that idle ceremony, to which our hearts were never
pledg'd ; which nature cancels, reason disavows,
and we both execrate religiously!—go where your
heart invites you : go to Dormer ; with him you
will be blest : with me each day, each hour will
aggravate your wretchedness.

LADY D. Can you be serious ?

LORD D. As death. The bitter moments you
have pass'd are sweet to those that must inevitably
follow.

LADY D. My Lord, my Lord, you put too
much upon me, when you urge me to a deed of
such disgrace. Your cruelty will shortly bring me
to my grave, then you'll be free ; but if the process be too slow for your impatience, draw forth
your sword ; I'll sooner meet its point, than be the
guilty thing that you would make me.

LORD D. Curst be these peevish scruples ! By
the Power that made me, if you will not accord to
my proposal, I will render life your torment !—and
for that bubble reputation, which you prize so
much above its worth, I'll blast it thro' the world :

I'll

I'll fasten shame upon you; it shall haunt you like your shadow: ridicule shall dog you at the heels: abuse and slander bark at you like hounds, and tear that virtue, which is but a cloak, to nakedness and rags: and when I've render'd you thus loathsome to behold, I'll take you at your word—bury my sword in your relentless breast, and after plunge it in my own.

LADY D. Alas, my Lord, I pity you, and feel more terror for your desperation than my own danger. There must be something horrid in your mind, more than you have yet disclos'd.

LORD D. Perhaps there is, and 'tis in pity that I call upon you now thus earnestly, thus for the last time, to save yourself. 'Tis not by nature I am cruel; one dishonourable deed, the impulse of a guilty passion, has distorted all my actions. I would confide it to you, for I hold you worthy every sacred trust, but —— . [*Paget Enters.*
Hah! he is come! bid Captain Dormer enter.

LADY D. Dormer again! then let me go.

LORD D. No, you must stay; by all that's sacred, you shall not depart.

LADY D. Support me, Heaven! and witness for me, that I did not seek this interview—'Tis he,

[*Enter Dormer; seeing Lady Davenant, he starts.*

LORD D. Stand not amaz'd, but enter: she whom you seek is here: the faded form, that once you thought so fair, is present.—Approach!

DORM. Yes, if my limbs will bear me—Oh! to each sense most dear!—thou best of women!
[*Advances to her.*

LORD D. Add too, unhappiest!

LADY D. Save me; support me, or I faint.
[*Dormer supports her in his arms.*

DORM. Help, help, my Lord! she faints.

LORD D. Alas! my touch will murder; be it your task; your right is preferable; for you she lov'd, me she only married.

DORM.

DORM. Can you look on unmov'd?

LORD D. How should you know what moves and passes here? I am the author of this interview:—It is the tribute of atonement. I am the man who counterfeited that letter that dismiss'd you from your hopes: the ship my interest procured for you, my jealousy provided—Now, if you wish destruction to your sister, give her in charge to me.

DORM. To infamy as soon. Return, and meet your death.   [*Lord Davenant is going.*

LORD D. Before you take my life, recover her's: when you've done that, I shall be found: mean time I leave with you my pledge.   [*Exit.*

LADY D. [*recovering*] What's that? where am I? ah! [*looking on Dormer, shrieks.*] O Dormer, Dormer!

DORM. Speak to me: unload your burthen'd heart: be candid to a friend, whose very soul is your's

LADY D. I had determin'd never to have seen you more.

DORM. O exemplary woman! even that I could have borne, had you been happy; but that monster shall not live.

LADY D. Hold, hold! you must not draw your sword upon Lord Davenant.

DORM. Not draw my sword! my wrongs and your redress will sanctify revenge: 'twere criminal to let him live.

LADY D. What! shall I be a party in the assassination of my husband?—I tell you, Dormer, if you ever draw your sword upon him, from that moment I renounce you; never will I see you, speak of you, or in meditation call you to remembrance, but with horror.

DORM. Not when he dares me to it?

LADY D. Never in any case, by any call or provocation, if you have love or pity for me left.

DORM. If I have love! oh, if the awful presence of your virtue did not check my tongue, I should have told you at your feet my uncontroll'd
                                        affection.

affection. If I have love, Louisa! notwithstanding your suppos'd unkindness, spite of all the artifices practis'd to estrange you from me, my unalter'd heart has still been your's: to the world's utmost limits I have carried your beloved image, the companion of each day, and the vision of each night: to the very gates of death it has attended me; it has chear'd me in sickness, cover'd me in battle, and been the guiding star, by which I shap'd my course.

LADY D. O Dormer, was it light affliction to a heart like mine to be depriv'd of all it held most dear? In the moment of my disappointment, when you, as I believed, renounc'd me, and departed without explanation, in that agony and conflict of my mind did they assail me, urge, compel me to a marriage with Lord Davenant. Why should I accuse him of unkindness? What could such a match produce but misery?—the efforts that I made to please him, though they cost me dear, could not impose on his sagacity; the labour'd tasks of duty poorly counterfeit the genuine glow of love.

DORM. Now then, Louisa, since your tyrant must escape unpunish'd, what do you resolve on? when he has left you to the world, where will you seek a shelter?

LADY D. Where can I shelter, but in my former asylum?

DORM. Go to the wretch that sacrificed you! No: what is this rigid arbiter, propriety, by whose decrees you are thus blindly govern'd?—what is this worldly idol, to whose bloody altars we must offer up our lives?

LADY D. What would you have me do? where would you have a wretched wife resort?

DORM. Is there no friend, whose faithful heart is your's?—what have I done, that I must be a second time excluded? I have a sister: may not she receive you?—my fortune now is ample—oh, reflect upon my sufferings, give me what honour can bestow—I ask no more.

LADY D. What shall I say?

DORM.

Dorm.　Do you still love me?

Lady D.　O Dormer, do not press me.

Dorm.　Nay, but resolve me—leave me not in doubt—my life is on your lips; silence will be my doom: I die, if you forbid it not.

Lady D.　Heaven and its blessed angels guard your life!

Dorm.　Do you still love me?

Lady D.　Dearer than life itself.

Dorm.　Give me a noble proof.

Lady D.　What wou'd you have me do?

Dorm.　Thus, thus for ever let me clasp you to my heart!—here let me hold you, This be your asylum! destin'd for each other, wedded in our souls, Heaven, that has re-united us, now sanctifies our privileg'd embrace. Spoil'd of my heart's best treasure, thus, my Louisa, by that dear lov'd name, thus, thus I claim thee:—now no tyrant husband, no base sordid uncle shall divide us more.

Enter Sir Edmund Travers, unperceiv'd.

Sir Edm.　Say you so, Sir? I'll try that point with you however——O scandal to your family! is this a situation for a wife to be found in?

Lady D.　No, I confess it;—your reproof is just.

Sir Edm.　Well, Sir, and this is honourable conduct, I suppose.　　　　[*to Dormer.*]

Dorm.　Sir Edmund Travers, I wou'd recommend it to you to keep your own temper, and not practise upon mine too far: And let me tell you, Sir, there is a mean and tricking quality in all you do. When hearts like ours are rent asunder by device and cunning—when forgery's base artifice is call'd in aid to separate affections, they will meet again, in spite of Hell itself: And if you have stolen by surprize upon that tender moment, when the most rigid virtue softens to endearment, beware of false conclusions; nor from the foulness of your own imagination, judge of ours.

Sir

Sir Edm. Fine talking! but as I have not out-
liv'd my senses; am in possession of my eyes and
ears; and have unluckily some interest in the reputation of my own niece, I shall take the liberty of
appealing to Lord Davenant against such proceeding.

Dorm. Madam, I do beseech you, undeceive
your uncle; I suspect he does not know the treat-
ment you receive; he could not else thus obstinately
persist to ruin you.

Lady D. Leave us together then, and I will
speak: retire into that room—nay, I request you:
will. [*Exit Dormer.*] Now give me patient hearing:—'tis not from consciousness of guilt, nor to
avoid a fair discussion of my sentiments for Captain Dormer, I wou'd wish you to desist; but from
a knowledge, which you have not, of Lord Davenant's disposition. You think him a kind husband;
—because I've troubled you with no complaints,
you think I've none to make: you are in an error;
and so long as error caus'd content, I left you in it;
now that it would lead to misery, I warn you of
its danger. My Lord and I are upon the point to
part: hitherto he has no shadow of complaint against
me; if you resolve to give him one, give this, report this indiscretion, swell it into criminality; perhaps he'll thank you for the office; but the time
will come, when you'll reproach yourself.

Sir Edm. And this you think will blind me;
—you mistake, I see your drift; I know you are
unhappy with your Lord, but I also know it is your
attachment to Dormer, and his return that make
you so; Lord Davenant told me so himself;—the
fault is all your own; you have driven him mad.
Now therefore, if you will solemnly engage your
word to me never to see Dormer again, I'll stifle
what is past; I'll still acknowledge you, protect
you; and if Lord Davenant then abandons you, I'll
receive you in my house—Now what do you say?
I put you to the proof.

Lady D.

LADY D. 'Tis fairly offer'd; but if every earthly comfort was in your difposel, and they cou'd only be obtain'd by my renouncing abfolutely and for ever all future friendly intercourfe with that much injur'd man, I wou'd reject 'em on fuch terms:——when I've faid this, I muft implore you not to pafs unfair conftructions on my refolution; for if you can ftill fufpect me, I will pledge my honour to you, never to receive his vifits, but in yours or other company :—will that content you?

SIR EDM. No, no, my Lady, nor cajole me neither; you'll not put out my eyes with duft; Nothing but abfolute renunciation of that villain will ferve me.

LADY D. Villain! do you call him villain?

SIR EDM. You'll find him fuch to you, incorrigible!——nay, I can now perfuade myfelf you have.

LADY D. To my Lord then with what difpatch you pleafe. Here comes your judge; prefer your charge againft me; I'll abide it.

Enter Lord Davenant.

SIR EDM. 'Tis well you are come, my Lord: I hope you will give me now a patient hearing.

LORD D. With fuch attention as a man, not over-ftor'd with patience, can command, I am prepar'd to hear you; When laft we met, you took me in a hafty moment; if I have offended you, impute it to infirmity, and now proceed.

SIR EDM. So, fo! he's quiet now; his phrenzy comes by fits. [*Afide.*] When I beftow'd this lady's hand in marriage to your Lordfhip, I had hope I gave you what would make your life a happy one; had it prov'd otherwife, I trufted that the fault wou'd not be hers; for fhe was born of worthy parents, carefully brought up, and educated in the habits of obedience.

LORD D. So much by way of preface; now to the point.

SIR

Sir Edm. Tho' she is under the dominion of a husband, still, as her uncle and her guardian, I am interested in her conduct; and when I meet her on the road to ruin——when I surprise her lock'd in the embraces of a lover——I hold it point of honour thus to bring her face to face, and put you on your guard.

Lord D. Lock'd in the embraces of a lover! of what lover?

Sir Edm. Dormer.

Lord D. Do you call him a lover?

Sir Edm. Can you make that a question? was he not ever such?——you know he was. She'll not deny it; question her yourself.

Lord D. I will not trouble you, Madam, with many interrogatories: be pleased to answer plainly. It is objected to you by your uncle that you love young Dormer.

Lady D. I have cause.

Sir Edm. Astonishing assurance! Have not I forbade you?——

Lord D. Be patient, if you please.——You loved him before you married me.

Lady D. I own it.

Lord D. You was trepanned into a marriage; not only forgery was employed, but force. Had you been left to choose, you would have chosen Dormer preferable to all mankind?

Lady D. I should.

Lord D. And was I now to die?——

Lady D. I beg you not to put that question?

Lord D. I shall forbear:——It does not need an answer.——Why, what a criminal you make yourself, Sir Edmund!——You an uncle! you a guardian!—you to conspire and league against a ward, whose happiness you had in charge!——For my share in the fraud, I do repent it from my soul; but have some excuse;——her beauty, fortune, were temptations in my way; ambition, avarice, desires might urge me on: mine was an interested baseness, yours a natural depravity!

Sir

SIR EDM. Heyday! the fit's returned; you are mad again: one and all mad. 'Tis the distemper of the times; it runs through the nation; hellebore can't stop it.

LORD D. Fly then before the infection catches you; keep the small wits you have at home, nor thrust yourself into the sphere of our infanity. When did you ever hear that interference between man and wife was thankfully received, or profitably answered any useful purpose?

SIR EDM. A word with you, madam, before we part:—Whatever happens, don't come near my doors; look not for your asylum there.   [*Exit.*

LORD D. Ridiculous old dotard! Suffer me to lead you to your chamber. your exhausted spirits must demand repose.   Give me your hand.

End of the Third A C T.

A C T   IV.

SCENE, *an Apartment in* Lord Davenant's *House.*

Charles Davenant and Dormer.

DAV. I HAVE now, Captain Dormer, told you without reserve the whole, as it has pass'd between your sister and myself, to the minutest circumstance; and I wait your answer, without foreseeing what that may be; for hitherto your silence has been such as gives no light to guess at your opinion.

DORM. I have heard your story with the deepest attention, for it involves the fortune of an orphan sister, in whose happiness I am closely interested and of whose reputation I am the rightful protector.

DAV.

Dav. If you find any cause of discontent in any proceeding, tell it me.

Dorm. I find no cause whatever for complaint ; but many, many proofs I find of generous manly honesty ;——and thus with open arms I take you to my heart, and lodge you there till it shall cease to beat. When I've said this, I must confess to you there are some painful incidents in your relation. My sister's marriage in Flanders I must consider as precipitate and rash ; the evidence of Brooke's disease at Paris was too readily admitted ; and the now distressful state of your engagement might have been avoided by those obvious precautions which your interest pointed out. Your marriage also is clandestine ; such are rarely happy ; and tho' Lord Davenant's consent would be no recommendation of it to me, methinks it should have been an indispensable preliminary to you.——

Dav. I feel the force of all you say. The vehemence of my affection may have out-slept prudence, and my want of confidence in my father may have violated duty, but towards your lovely sister I should hope I stand without reproach.

Dorm. I cannot doubt your honour, and you'll suffer me to add, there does not live a man on earth I should be so proud to call my brother. Here we must pause—till we have trac'd the villain out who has abus'd her confidence, and by a feign'd decease plung'd her and you in this distress and doubt ; no self-indulging passion must be suffer'd to complete the yet suspended marriage—this promise you will make ?

Dav. And keep religiously—As for discovery, his equipage I hope will lead to that.

Dorm. Perhaps it will ; if that should be the case, remember, Captain Davenant, 'tis to me he must account. Now I'll go to my sister.

Dav. Do so :—I am sure I need not warn you to speak tenderly to Marianne : commend me to her, cheer her gentle spirits, and assuage, if possible, her anxious thoughts in this uneasy crisis.

E   Dorm.

Dorm.. I'll do my beſt; but ſtill my heart is heavy. Fare you well!   [*Exit.*

Enter Lady Davenant.

Lady D. Was not that Dormer?

Dav. It was.

Lady D. You have told him of your marriage?

Dav. I have.

Lady. D. Well, and how paſs'd it? I'm impatient to be told that you at leaſt are happy.

Dav. Happy! alas—

Lady D. What ails you? what has diſconcerted you? you have no miſunderſtanding ſure with Dormer?

Dav. With Dormer none.

Lady D. Your father then?

Dav. I have not ſeen him: this it. is:—I told you Marianne had made a former marriage in Flanders; that her huſband after three months left her, went to Paris, and there died. She thought herſelf a widow; till this morning after I had left you, and with tranſport flew to embrace my bride, I found her bath'd in tears and agoniz'd with grief;—the impoſtor had deceiv'd her; he was living;—ſhe had ſeen her huſband.

Lady, D. Oh horrible! her huſband living! ——how have you ſupported it? what is become of her; of Dormer?—where will this affliction end?

Dav. I know not; I am now in ſearch of the betrayer.

Lady D. Have you no clue to trace him by?

Dav. I think we have; and from a circumſtance that I omitted to relate.——How now? what news?

[*A Servant enters, and ſpeaks aſide to Davenant.*

Lady D. Poor Davenant! how I pity thee! ſure I had weight ſufficient of affliction. How ſhall a ſorrow-broken heart ſupport ſuch overwhelming grief?

Dav.

Dav. '[*To the Servant.*] Go to your Lady: tell her all is well. You'll find her brother with her Captain Dormer ; take him aside, and tell him to repair to me without a moment's loss : your diligence ; shall be rewarded. Go ; make haste. [*Exit Servant.* Now the discovery's out—I told you Marianne had seen her husband ; his chariot passing her window was stopt by accident in the street ; the mob and clamour usual on such occasions attracted her notice and that of the neighbours : my servant now informs me 'twas the equipage of Sir Harry Harlow.

Lady D. What do you say ? Sir Harry Harlow's !—no ; it must not be. Revoke that word.

Dav. Revoke it ! why should I revoke it ? no, I'll drag him to detection.

Lady D. When did that pass, do you say ? was it this morning, after you saw me ?

Dav. It was ; I told you that before :—what interests you so deeply for Sir Harry Harlow ?

Lady D. What interests me ! what !—O Charles ——forbear to question me—it stabs my heart :—I do beseech you leave me to myself :—It turns my brain. Give me a minute's recollection.

[*Walks aside.*

Dav. Now by my soul, 'tis very strange : it staggers me. Suspicions force upon me : nothing is more evident than her disorder : it smote her like a stroke of death—nay, 'tis most palpable : her eyes are staring wild with horror. Ah ! 'tis so ; she loves him. Curse upon him ! he has prevail'd with her too.—Heavens ! what a character is overthrown !

[*Aside.*

Lady D. Charles, Charles, you must be patient in this business. Do not trust your information too implicitly ; nor hurry on an explanation that you may repent of.

Dav. Must I be patient, Madam ? must I permit the direst villain to survive ?—and do you plead for him ?—no, if my honour was not pledg'd to Dormer not to take up this affair, without him, by my soul a moment shou'd not pass before my sword shou'd make its passage to the traitor's heart !

E 2 Lady

LADY D. What traitor's heart? you must not
call him traitor.

DAV. Amazement! Lady Davenant, you con-
found me:—'tis too flagrant. Have I not proof certain?

LADY D. No, no; I tell you, wretched man,
you have no proof—and when you have—

DAV. What then!—why then I'd drag him from
the altar: stab him, tho' your fond arms protected
him.

LADY D. You don't know what you say.

DAV. 'Tis you that say you know not what;—
'tis you, alas! whom this confusion painfully betrays;
—you, whom a fatal weakness forces to protect the
blackest of mankind. By Heaven that gave me life,
I thought you late a miracle of truth and goodness:
I approach'd you with a reverence that border'd on
idolatry. I leave you now with mournful pity and
regret; I go, because I can no longer bear to be
spectator of the fall of such exalted virtue. [*Exit.*

Lady Davenant.

LADY D. Lost, lost, for ever lost!—go, miserable youth; enjoy the respite of a short mistake:
the moment that clears up my innocence, lets fall
despair on thee: what a tremendous scene will that
unfold! a father husband to thy wife!—It must be
so: a multitude of circumstances now confirm it;
—this, this it is that solves the mystery of his unna-
tural conduct: this is the latent dagger of his mind:
this is his horror: this the injury so unatoneable to
Dormer. The very hour in which he took Sir Harry's equipage; his journey to the continent; his stay
abroad, and his long silence, whilst in absence from
me, rise in horrible array, a host of witnesses, de-
posing to the dreadful truth. Inextricable distress!
what can be done? I see no light:—Fate labours
as with mother's pangs, and the fell babe of horror,
hell-begotten, presses to the birth—Father of mer-
cies, give me thy support!——Without there! who
attends?

Enter

Enter Servant.

Is your Lord still at home ?

SERV. My Lord is in the library with Sir Harry Harlow.

LADY D. Has Captain Davenant been there ?

SERV. No, Madam, he has this moment left the house.

LADY D. Run to my Lord, tell him to give no-body admittance till I have seen him; and desire Sir Harry Harlow to come hither immediately. [*Exit Servant.*] I am not in the fault: I have not driven him to this desperate act. Be witness for me, truth, I have not wilfully occasion'd his disgust, but studied to my utmost to obey and please him. If by Sir Harry's means I can hold off this fatal explanation, till Lord Davenant takes his measures, an interview perhaps may be avoided that is horrible to think of——I sent to you, Sir Harry.

Enter Sir Harry Harlow.

SIR H. H. I flew with ardour at your summons; and I await your pleasure, with a heart that throbs to serve you—with a heart, dear Lady, that can only cease to love, when it shall cease to beat.

LADY D. 'Tis well; I mean to put your friend-ship to the proof.

SIR H. H. Friendship indeed! but call it by what name you will; my life is yours; command it to what purpose you see fit.

LADY D. Pray don't mistake yourself or me—You lent your chariot to my Lord this morning ?—

SIR H. H. Madam!—

LADY D. Come, come, I know you did: I saw it at my door: I saw him enter it.

SIR H. H. Then I must not dispute the point with you ;—to any other question I yield no answer.

LADY D. 'Twill be a service most essential to my happiness, if you will consent to screen Lord Davenant for a while; I wou'd not put this on you,

but

but for most pressing reasons ; nor do I mean that
any risque or imputation thence arising shou'd ulti-
mately fall on you : therefore, I do beseech you for
an hour or so that you will be invisible to all enquiries, but above all to Captain Dormer and Charles
Davenant. Return not to my Lord, but quit this
house immediately ; and if I might prevail, you
shou'd not enter your own for some time ; they'll
seek you there, and if their fury shall compel you to
an explanation, I must tremble for the consequences.

Sir H. H. Most amiable of women !—I perceive your drift : you act too nobly by an undeserv-
ing husband ; but I make no appeal ; implicitly I
shall obey, because 'tis your command ;—and tho'
my life were made the sacrifice, what were more
glorious than to die for you ?—one word, one kind
approving look can overpay the purchase ; grant
that before we part, and at your feet I dedicate for
ever to your service my devoted heart.

Enter Davenant hastily, followed by Dormer.

Dav. Villain, stand up, and answer me. Now,
Dormer, now will you believe me ? Have we found
you, Sir ?

Dorm. Draw, wretch, for I am Dormer.

                                    [*He does not draw.*

Lady D. You are mad : or sheath your sword,
or pass its murderous point thro' me.

Dorm. O shame, shame, shame ! and have I
liv'd to see it ? O mortal blow to modesty !—Let
there be no fidelity in woman, no faith henceforth
in man !—Come forth, thou shelter'd coward ! answer with thy life : it is not for thine own enor-
mities alone, 'tis for hers also thou must now account.

Sir H. H. I'll answer nothing, but to every
tittle of your charge to say 'tis grossly false. Settle
your own precedencies ;—I am ready.

Lady D. Will you hear reason ? Dormer,
Charles, I do conjure you both, forbear !

                                            Sir

SIR H. H. Give their rage way: they chuse a notable occasion in a lady's presence to display their valour!

DORM. Our Wrongs are such as will not bear delay; nor will we trust to one who can change names, shift persons, counterfeit even death itself to ruin innocence and mock avenging justice.

SIR H. H. I don't know what you say; but such affassin-like attacks deserve no answer, nor admit of any explanation. You, Mr. Davenant, know me well; you know I, may and will be found:—appoint your place, I'll meet you.

DAV. Follow us then!—

LADY D. Help, help!—You shall not stir.—This is too much.—You are deceiv'd; he's innocent.—help, help!

[Runs to the door, and meets Lord Davenant.

Enter Lord Davenant.

LORD D. What is this uproar? who has frighted you?—Hah! Dormer here?—Sir Harry, what has pass'd?

SIR H. H. Pass'd, my Lord! nothing; all is mystery to me.

LORD D. Why did she scream out?—A word with you. *[Takes Sir H. H. aside.*

DAV. [To Dormer.] Dormer, contain yourself; there's something here that's dark and terrifying: say nothing to my father;—let us withdraw, and wait below; there can be no escape. Nay, follow me, I do conjure you.

DORM. O Lady Davenant, reconcile my mind to this mysterious conduct, or break my heart at once. *[Exit with Davenant.*

LADY D. What then becomes of mine? it bursts distracted with o'erwhelming grief.

SIR H. H. Look to my Lady.—

LADY D. No, no; regard not me; I shall not fail; Heaven sends me strength for my appointed task. ——Let me be private with you.

[To Lord Davenant.

LORD

LORD D. Not for the world:—my thoughts
are terrible; I am possess'd by fiends—stay, and be
witness to my shame, whilst I confess the black ac-
compt which I must pass with Dormer: I have betray'd his sister; ruin'd her by forgeries and false-
hoods, as I did you, Louisa;—married her.

SIR H. H. Infamous deed!

LORD D. Yes, Sir, there is rebellion in my
blood; his sword must let it out:—therefore no
more, but let me pass.

[*As he is going out, Lady Davenant stops him.*

LADY D. Hold, hold! you must not stir.

LORD D. What is't—you mean? why do you
cross me thus?

LADY D. To save you from a meeting worse
than death.

LORD D. To save your lover from a meeting
that may lead to death.——Oh! whilst you live,
speak truth:——'tis love of Dormer raises this alarm.
Have I not found the cause?

LADY D. No, you've not found the cause:——
wou'd that you never could!

SIR H. H. Be caution'd by your Lady, and
impute to her concern no other than the purest motive;——my life upon it, you will find it such.
Alas, unhappy man, what treasure have you cast
away? Hear her, console her, be advis'd by her:
recover, if you can, her forfeited esteem. She is
a miracle of goodness.

LORD D. Dost think me so far sunk in honour,
as to shrink from this discussion? Dormer's en-
titled to an honourable satisfaction, and I shall
give it him immediately. Before we part however, Lady Davenant, let me own that I am pe-
netrated with remorse for my conduct to you. Tho'
I ask nothing for myself, I am not out of hope that
you will cast an eye of pity and protection on that
guiltless sufferer, who, if I fall, will be the part-
ner of your widowhood:——she is young and beau-
tiful; and if your influence over Dormer is exerted

in

in her favour, she may retrieve the unhappy error
into which I led her.——Farewel!

LADY D. Yet, yet prevent him——Stay;——
she has a husband.

LORD D. What do you tell me? speak that
word again.

LADY D. She has a husband——and that husband——how shall I pronounce it?——

LORD D. Go on: I'll have it, tho' it breathes
destruction.

LADY D. That husband is your son.

LORD D. Death to my soul!——My son!

LADY D. Your son this morning married Dormer's sister.

LORD D. Why do I live a moment?

[*Lays his Hand on his Sword.*

SIR H. H. Stop your rash hand.——What phrenzy seizes you?

LORD D. Why does the earth not yawn, and
whelm me to the centre?——Oh what a day of
dreadful retribution!——Why was this marriage
secret?——which of you was privy to it?

LADY D. I knew it not, nor had suspicion of
it:——few hours are past since he disclos'd it to
me.

LORD D. Fatal concealment!——horrible event!
——O God, O God, into what misery have I
plung'd my son!——Does he know what I have
done?

SIR H. H. Nor he nor Dormer know it.——take
this comfort also to your heart; it is as yet a marriage but in form: the day is not yet passed, in
which their hands were join'd.——Heaven in its
vengeance has remember'd mercy.

LORD D. Call my son here directly.

LADY D. There let me interpose again. Take
a short time for serious meditation: we will assist
your thoughts. Your friend here has already struck
one spark of light amidst your dark despair; patient
reflection may bring more in view. Perhaps this
meeting with your son, which you in your mind's

present agitation are for hastening, prudence may postpone.

Lord D. Speak on, for there is something in your voice like comfort; something that falls upon my ear, like music in the dead of night after distressful dreams.

Lady D. Oh! if a few calm words can lull your ear, think how repentance may assuage your soul:——for so much of your offence as falls on me alone, I thank Heaven's mercy for its aid, I can forgive it; nay, my Lord, I have forgiven it.

Lord D. Nay, but you must abhor me; darkness must be less opposite to light, than I to innocence:——so loathsome am I to myself, I shou'd despise the person that cou'd pity me.

Sir H. H. Come to your chamber; follow your guardian angel where she leads you:——If I can serve you in this melancholy hour, command me; if I am in your way, dismiss me.

Lord D. I pray you leave me not——I have a thing to tell you——It is not known to man, nor can your heart conceive, how dire a deed I've had in meditation:——there was a thought struck on my mind too terrible for utterance: but it is past: this stroke, that cuts up all resource of hope, cuts up the bloody purpose that I had in hand. And now I feel as it were two natures:—my good and evil genius seem at strife within me; this touches me with human kindness and remorse; that tears me with despair and horror. How it will end I know not; for all command is lost, and my mind drives like a wreck before the tempest.——Go with my Lady Davenant; stay by her, I beseech you. I will retire to my chamber. Farewell!

[Exeunt severally.

End of the Fourth ACT.

ACT

A C T   V.

An Apartment in Lord Davenant's *House.*

Dormer discovered alone.

DORM. 'TIS near an hour I have waited here, and still this man appears not. I should suspect he had escap'd me, if Davenant had not positively said, there was no other way for him to pass but thro' this room. No solitude can be more silent than the House:——they are in conference still. My mind is on the rack; I am tortur'd with uncertainty——He comes——My Lady Davenant!

Enter Lady Davenant.

LADY D. Is your friend yet return'd?

DORM. No, Madam; Captain Davenant is not yet come back.

LADY D. But you expect him soon?

DORM. With every moment. Has your Ladyship any thing in command for him that I can deliver?

LADY D. No, Sir: my servants have my orders, when he comes, to beg that I may see him instantly. *[Going.*

DORM. Stop, I beseech you, for a moment stop! is it with him alone you will confer? am I not worthy of a word? a look?——or will you turn, but when Sir Harry kneels?

LADY D. Yes; I wou'd turn to Dormer, cou'd I see him.

DORM. Am I not Dormer? is he not before you?

LADY D. To memory he is present, not to sight. The picture of him in my mind is clear and spotless, trac'd with benevolence and truth and courage.; it beams with candour, and it glows with love.——The picture in my eye is false and faded, smear'd by some spurious dawber, patcht, distorted; the open smile of honour wrinkled to a leer of livid jealousy——a libel, not a likeness of a man. [*Exit.*

DORM. Hear only what I have to offer: stay, and hear me:——she's gone and gives no ear: unjust, disdainful!——Hah! by my hopes, her scorn shall be repay'd——her paramour approaches—— You are found, Sir——

Enter Sir Harry Harlow.

At last we are alone; and tho'-I find you under Lady Davenant's roof, yet your protectress being absent, that shall no longer be your safeguard.

SIR H. H. I own I wish'd to have avoided you; but since we are met, proceed to state your charge.

DORM. No wonder you shou'd wish to avoid me, for you have done a base unmanly injury to a defenceless orphan; by a pretended generosity you stole into her good opinion, married and abandoned her. Base as this is, there is a meanness in the act, that makes it more detestable than open villainy—— you counterfeited death; paltry expedient! which not only gives your tongue the lie, but stamps it on your life.—Draw then! defend yourself; for 'tis not now a counterfeited death, but the reality, that must determine one of us.

SIR H. H. Take your own course; I shall repel assault: but first, by way of caution, hear me:—— 'Twas once my chance, as it is now, to be call'd out by a rash angry boy, to answer with my sword for an imputed injury to a lady, whom he took on himself to protect. I met him, for his rage was deaf to reason: being master of the sword, I soon disarm'd my hot antagonist:—when I had given him life, I gave him proof of his mistake:—the youth was satisfied.

tisfied, and fav'd. A fecond inftance may not be fo happy.

DORM. I underftand you; but the proofs, which in this inftance follow'd, now precede our interview. You'll not deny the equipage was your's; that you was in it; that my fifter faw you, call'd out to you to ftop: you did; but, looking out, difcover'd her, and bafely took to flight?—thefe facts bring home to you unanfwerable proof, and leave you nothing but confeffion and atonement.

SIR H. H. This arrogance compels me to an act, which, in compaffion to your youth, and the misfortunes that hang over it, I fain would have avoided. I draw my fword, not to anfwer to your charge, but to chaftife your infult:—Still I bear fo little of revenge about me, that if you'll fatisfy my honour with the leaft apology, I promife you an hour fhall not pafs before I'll clear my innocence.

DORM. That you can never do; for if by any palliation you could hope to fmooth away your injuries to my fifter, ftill their remains a black account of crimes, which nothing but your life can expiate: Thefe eyes have feen you at the feet of Lady Davenant.

SIR H. H. Stop your blafpheming tongue!— die, madman, in your error! [*They pafs at each other.*

Marianne runs in, followed by Davenant.

MAR. Hold, for the love of Heaven!—Charles, Charles, beat down their fwords! See, fee, my brother bleeds. *Charles interpofes.*

DORM. 'Tis but a fcratch—Stand off!

MAR. What is your quarrel? Why does he affault you?

DORM. Can you afk that? has your fright blinded you? do you not recollect that face?

MAR. I never to my knowledge faw that gentleman before.

F DAV.

DAV. I did suspect this, Dormer; and on that account I brought your sister with me.

DORM. Have patience if you please——Come hither, Marianne, look at that gentleman: Do you forget, or will you not acknowledge your husband?

MAR. Husband! I tell you he's a perfect stranger.

DORM. If you say this from fear, or false respect for what may follow to affect my safety, you do wrong both to yourself and me: therefore I charge you answer me sincerely and without disguise.

MAR. As Heaven shall judge me I have spoke the truth.

DORM. I'm satisfied:——Sir Harry Harlow, I perceive my error; and for so much as affects this Lady, I sincerely ask your pardon.

SIR H. H. So much for one of your mistakes; there is another, which you must atone for:——a little patience will clear all; reserve your spirits for that trial;——you now conceive the reason why my Lady Davenant interpos'd in my behalf: she knew my innocence, and therefore stopt your hand; when you know hers, the sword you pointed at my breast, take care you turn it not upon your own: none but the same defender can preserve you.

DORM. I own, the circumstance of this mistake has clear'd that part of Lady Davenant's conduct; it only now remains to account why you was found upon your knees before her.

SIR H. H. How else should I approach her? When you know all her virtues, you will worship too:——the presence of an angel must demand our knees.——But you are wounded, Sir; you bleed.

DORM. 'Tis nothing; a mere scratch; your point just glanc'd upon my arm.

SIR H. H. 'Tis well it is no worse. Good night to you! [*Going.*

DAV. Before you go, one word with you, Sir Harry——I am certainly inform'd the person we are now in search of was in your chariot this morning,

ing, when an accident ſtopt it in the ſtreet where this Lady lives: I demand of you as a man of honour to inform me who that Perſon is.

SIR H. H. When you take that for granted, Charles, which I have not admitted, and thereon ground a queſtion I'm not bound to anſwer, you muſt give me leave to ſay, you have already had the only ſatisfaction I ſhall give. I have been once arraing'd, am now acquitted, and ſhall no longer plead to interrogatories.

DAV. Permit me then to tell you, Sir—

SIR. H. H. No, tell me nothing I ought not to hear; for I regard you much too well to ſtart a quarrel with you; rather let me tell you, Charles, what you ſhould hear, and thank me for— you and your friend there have arraing'd a lady perfect in all goodneſs, conſtruing the pureſt motives into criminality. I ſee her coming, and ſhall leave you this fair opportunity, to make atonement: When you have done that, if you have any farther difference, to compoſe with me, I ſhall attend your call when, where, and how you pleaſe.   [*Exit.*

Enter Lady Davenant.

DAV. But that I know your heart, I ſhould deſpair of pardon; ſuffer me to hope you will forgive, my moſt unjuſt ſuſpicion, and receive into your favour my beloved Marianne.

LADY D. This is the Lady—if I ſurvey her for a while with melancholy admiration I ſhall not offend; is this a form to combat rude misfortune? that it ſhould enter in the heart of a man to injure ſuch a creature! that artifice and wrong might be employ'd to gain her I can comprehend, but that they ſhould be a reſource for leaving her, ſurpaſſes my conception: I find till now Imagination could not reach the guilt of her betrayer.—Give me your hand, my dear, you come into a melancholy houſe: I cannot welcome you as I would wiſh.

MAR. And cauſe there is for melancholy: whereever I am preſent, it purſues me: I am the bitter

fountain

fountain of your sorrow. My fatal Marriage with this noble youth has been the bane and poison of your peace I pray you send me hence; dismiss me like a thing abhorr'd; a pestilence, that, if you harbour it, will pay your hospitality with death.

LADY D. Not so; misfortune strengthens your interest in my heart. You have more claims upon me than you know of. You are still married in your heart to Davenant; so was I once to Dormer.

DORM. Oh! I shall sink with shame.

LADY D. Had I been, as you are, thus wretched, thus betray'd, nor wife nor widow, but a nameless 'orphan, the sport of villany, affliction's victim—you had a brother once, in whose brave heart I shou'd have rais'd that pity you excite in mine.

DORM. Oh, plead for me, some friend! I dare not speak.

LADY D. No, Dormer, no: when I forgive, you shall not owe it to an advocate: but let that rest; things of more moment press.—You must not see your father. [*to Davenant.*]

DAV. Why not? your words alarm me.

LADY D. His situation would alarm you more: some strange disorder suddenly has seiz'd him.

DAV. Say rather some strange passion of the mind. —You told him of my marriage?—

LADY D. I did, and he receiv'd it like a stroke of death; his frame convuls'd with passion.—I must for ever lament your not consulting him.

DAV. Does he resent it highly?

LADY D. We'll talk of that hereafter; for the present you must avoid an interview. If you remain in the house, retire to your own chamber, and let her accompany you;—take Mr. Dormer with you too—Go, my dear child, go with your friend—so you may call him still.

MAR. My heart's too full to utter what it feels. —In the expressive language of your eyes I read my melancholy fate.—Farewel!

[*Exit with Davenant.*

LADY D. Well. Sir, you'll follow that unhappy pair;—or do you wait to spring some new detection?—Fie upon you!—What blemish does your scrutinizing eye discover, that you so stedfastly peruse me over?—Oh, that a taint so sickly as suspicion should find admittance in a hero's breast!

DORM. [*runs to Lady Davenant, and falls at her feet*] Hear me, divine Louisa, hear your repentant Dormer:—let me kneel for pardon.

LADY D. Rise, rise!—this is no time for explanation.

DORM. Stop not my words, now they have found their way, but let me pour them and my tears, thus kneeling at your feet.—Before my eyes lose sight of you, confirm my pardon: tell me you forgive what my impatient phrenzy, what my mad suspicion utter'd—Penitence ne'er struck a human heart more deep than mine.—Dæmons have curs'd the sun, I have done more—I have arraign'd thy virtue.

LADY D. Rise, I desire you, rise! you have my full forgiveness.

DORM. Oh! first and last sole object of my heart! how can I thank thee as I ought?
[*Kisses her hand.*

LADY D. If to regain and keep your place in my affection is your wish, spare the attempt to thank me, nor by this warmth of passion draw aside my thoughts from the sad theme that fills them. That I have lov'd you, Dormer, and still love, superior to disguise, accept my free confession; but when example meets me of the precipitancy of passion in Davenant's case; of the deceitfulness of gratitude in Marianne's; I will be guided only by esteem; and on your delicacy, on your discretion in this mournful crisis will depend, if that affection which I now acknowledge shall subsist or cease. [*Exeunt.*

Enter Lord Davenant and Paget,

LORD D. The air is fresher here: motion revives me.

PAGET.

PAGET. I wish it may: and yet your colour changes; your eyes look heavy, and betoken pain.

LORD D. I've wearied them with writing. Take the papers—This to my son; to Lady Davenant this; and this to Dormer.——Ah!

PAGET. What's that? another pang?—and now it shakes you like an ague fit: pray be persuaded; let your physician be sent for.

LORD D. What can he do? my wounds are in the soul. Give me your arm.

PAGET. How cold your hand is on me!

LORD D. No matter: 'twill pass off.—I'm better now. Make all things ready. I will be gone to night.

PAGET. How can you travel with these pains upon you?

LORD D. I shall feel no pains upon my journey.

PAGET. I fear, my Lord, you are not fit to undertake your journey.

LORD D. I fear so too: but, be that as it may, let me have all things ready. Have you put up those parchments for my son?

PAGET. They are in the box, seal'd and directed—or Mr. Davenant..

LORD D. That's very well—now tell my Lady that I desire to see her.—A word with you before you go:—You will find I have not forgot your services; they would have done credit to a better cause; but as I have put you above necessity, I hope I have put you above meanness also.

PAGET. It has not been my choice, but my misfortune. I shall send Lady Davenant to you, and hope she will prevail with you to postpone your journey. [*Exit.*

Lord Davenant.

LORD D. My journey must be quickened, not postponed —This medicine works too slowly;—but here's a remedy of more dispatch:—Apply it then! —Misery like mine acquits the suicide; when law

strikes

strikes short, justice should arm the culprit's hand.
—The occasion's apt:—In death there's but one
pang, in life a thousand thousand multiplied cala-
mities.—Now, now I'll do it.—Hah! I'm inter-
rupted.

Enter Lady Daveranst.

LADY D. I am told you have been seized with
sudden indisposition;——what is the matter?——
How are you affected?——Are you resolved upon
departing immediately?

LORD D. I am resolved; my mind is gone before me; and when I am departed, I shall bequeath
you to your heart's first choice.

LADY D. What do you meditate?——Your
words, your looks are ominous. What was that
thing you huddled in your bosom, as I entered?—
My Lord, my Lord, beware of self destruction!——
Your bosom labours, your breath flutters, and your
eyes———Oh horrible! what are these ghastly symp-
toms?

LORD D. If any consolation could have rescued
me, thine would have been the medicine of my
mind;——thou would'st have been 'the saving angel,
thou most excellent, most injured of women!——
But I have sate in council with my reason, ransack'd
all the resources of my soul, and questioned every
rising thought, if it could show me hope:——In all
my composition, there is not one trace; night and
despair possess me, and there is nothing like a ray
of light, save only what the mortal drug admi-
nisters, that now is sapping the strong-hold of life.

LADY D. Poison!——Oh let me fly and bring
you instant help.

LORD D. Hold, I command you:——Assistance
is too late; nor would I suffer it, if it came.——
'Sdeath! I were a beast without a soul;——I that
have kept my station with the highest, now to sink
where infamy won't own me;——the outcast of
society, the pointing-stock of scorn, and feed on
offal

offal fcraps of pity, thrown by charitable fools, to comfort me!——it is not to be borne!——Defpair feized me, and I took poifon.

LADY D. Be not extreme with him in judgment, merciful Difpofer!——He comes, but not in confidence :——defpair compels him.

LORD D. I thank you.——O Louifa! beft of woman!——if I had confidence to pray, it fhould be for fuch bleffings on your future days, as might redeem and recompence your fufferings paft. And yet I'll ftrive——Oh horrible! it muft not be.—— My foul is rent with agony :——Methought, as I looked up, I faw a thoufand threatening faces, that forbade my prayer. Oh hide me in your arms!—— Stand off again! left I infeċt and ftain your purity with my unholy touch.——Bleft may you be! thrice bleft in Dormer's arms!——May heaven fhower down on your united hearts perpetual harmony and love! And for the hateful barrier of my life, thus, thus I burft it———

[*Stabs himfelf, and fhe catches his arm.*
LADY D. Ah!

LORD D. Let go my arm! my foul is in a loathfome prifon, and this ftroke delivers it.

[*Stabs again, and drops on one knee, holding*
the dagger ftill in his hands.
LADY D. Help! for the love of Heaven, fome help!

Enter Davenant and at another door Servants.

O Charles your! father has deftroy'd himfelf.

DAV. Merciful God! he is dying.

LADY D. The agonies of death are on him. Affift me to take him off:——I can't fupport him; ——he will die upon the floor.

LORD. D. Yes, yes, 'tis over!——tell not my fon the caufe till I am dead. This was the only kindnefs I could fhew him. I am forry to prefent a fpectable fo bloody to you both: but poifon work'd too fluggifhly, nor could I bear its agonies

——oh

———oh keep her from the fight of me!———she
comes———

Enter Marianne, followed by Dormer.

MAR. What have we here? Oh horrible! what
dying man is this?

LORD D. Oh hide me! cover me with clouds:
I fink, I die——have pity for me, Heaven!———
'tis paft.   [*Dies.*

MAR. Let me come to him: let me fee his
face. 'Tis he! avenging Heaven! it is my hufband.

DORM. Lord Davenant your Hufband! ——com-
plicated mifery!

DAV. her hufband and my father?

LADY D. The Horrid myftery is folv'd.

MAR. Then let me die;——let my heart burft
at once, and bury me for ever in oblivion.

LADY D. No, whilft my arms, my friendfhip
can uphold you, you fhall never fall.——Come
from the body, Charles:——ceafe to contemplate
that bloody object.

DAV. Nay, but be filent——it is done——he's
dead——I will be dumb henceforth; but have
fome care of me, for if my reafon fails, and not
remembering he was my father, I fhould fhock nature's hearing with a curfe, 'twill be the brain's depravity, and not the heart's.

LADY D. Alas, unhappy friends, my fpirits will
not ferve to give you confolation; but let us pati-
ently await, and it will come from Heaven:——
the fame difpenfing hand, that to the blamelefs bo-
fom deals the wound, will in its own good time
adminifter the cure.

F I N I S.

EPILOGUE.

SPOKEN BY MISS YOUNGE.

TO-night two sketches we've held up to view,
One of the old school, t'other of the new.
As for my Lady's portrait, I can't boast
Its likeness, for the original is lost:
In times foregone the colouring might be good,
But now it scarce resembles flesh and blood:
The pencil's chaste—but where I would demand,
Are the soft touches of a modern hand?
Where the fond languish that our matters steal?
The tempting bosom that our dames reveal?
Where the high plume that speaks the towering soul?
Where the bright glofs that varnishes the whole?
The Habit regimental, smart cockade,
And the neat ankle roguishly displayd'?
None, none of these—a peice of mere still life,
Where not one feature marks the modern wife.

Lay the good dame aside—and now behold
My Lord appears!—These tints are fresh and bold;
This is the life itself.   Mark what a grace
Beams in his high-born tyranny of face!
He breathes; he speaks.   Cards, harlots, horses, dice
Croud the back-ground with attributes of vice:
This, this is something like; these colours give
Some semblance of a man: *'Tis so we live.*
'Tis so we look, you cry—behold once more!
The suicide is welt'ring in his gore
Ha! does it strike you? say, do you still cry,
'Tis so we live?—so live, and so you'll die.

But one word more on *Lady Davenant's* part,
We hope 'tis nature; you believe it Art,
Search your own bosoms; if you find her there
'Tis well: if not, I wou'd to heaven she were!